04-02-22

**For everyone who needs
(and needed) Sid and Spencer.**

ISBN 979-8-9856631-0-5 (Hardcover)

SPENCER'S NOISY MIXER

PAIGE AMANDA

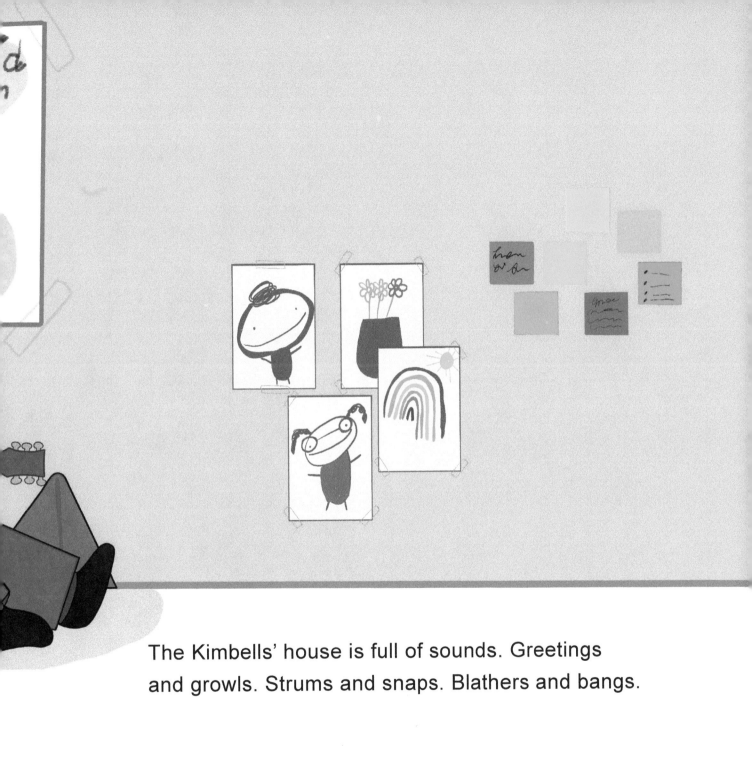

The Kimbells' house is full of sounds. Greetings
and growls. Strums and snaps. Blathers and bangs.

The Kimbell siblings, Sid and Spencer,
were the primary noisemakers.

Sid loved zooming scooter boards,

snarling lions,

and knocking down block structures.

Most of all, they loved to roar!

ROOAAR!

Spencer loved jumping,

humming,

and baking soft, chewy things that made her hum with happiness when she ate them.

Baking was Spencer's special interest. She wanted to bake every day. For her birthday, she got a brand new stand mixer. Sid was intrigued by the new gadget until the mixer started whirring and burring.

Sid roared at it to stop. Spencer just kept mixing, hyperfocused on creating the perfect cookie consistency.

Sid fell to the ground, toppling Spencer's mixing bowl.
Spencer screamed, and everyone ended up crying.

Afterward, the Kimbells' usually
noisy house went silent.

Once everyone had calmed down,
Mama asked Sid what happened.

At a loss for words, Sid
pointed at the mixer.
They groaned and clutched
their head.

"It seems like the mixer is
hurting your body."
said Mama. "We need to make
sure everyone is safe.
Spencer, maybe you
could use the mixer
only when Sid isn't
downstairs."

Spencer thought about the meringue cookies she was making. She needed the mixer to get perfect stiff peaks. She also thought about how often Sid was in the same room as her. She shook her head no.

"This is a tricky situation," said Mama.

After some time, Sid shouted, "I just need a helmet for my ears!"

That got Mama thinking. "A helmet for your ears? I think they make something like that."

Both siblings looked at each other in disbelief.

"I'll be right back." Mama raced off.

When she returned, she was holding the ear defenders that she wears when she can't find her earplugs.

"I think we should get some of these for you, Sid."

"Can I still be a lion with those ear helmets on, Mama?" Sid asked worriedly.

"How about you try them on to find out?" suggested Mama, handing Sid the ear defenders.

Sid put on the ear defenders and let out a roar. Sid realized that they could hear their growls even more clearly than before! It was almost as if they were actually on the savannah.

Sid excitedly picked out some
bright yellow ear defenders.

OUTSIDE

INSIDE

They waited as patiently as they could.

Finally, a special package
arrived just for them.

And with some
adjustments...

ROOAAR!

Sid's ear defenders were ready to protect.

From then on, with the help of their trusty ear defenders, Sid was able to safely watch Spencer use her mixer.

The Kimbells' house is still full of sounds.

But now, everyone gets to control the volume.

Author's note

Spencer's Noisy Mixer isn't a story that existed when I was a kid. Still, even as I write this in 2022, the lack of books written by and for Autistic folks is stark. And books about Autistics of color? Incredibly rare. But Spencer's Noisy Mixer isn't just a book about representation. It is a book that intentionally reframes conversations around Autism. It was important to me that I tell a story that is informed by respectful parenting and the unique knowledge that comes from Autistic adults. We *were* Autistic children after all. Too much of the information available to caregivers harms and stigmatizes neurodivergent children by attempting to "fix" instead of accomodate them. This is beginning to change as Autistics and our allies continue to share neurodiversity affirming knowledge. With this book, I hope to help shape a world that loves and accepts neurodivergent children as they are.

Consider how Sid and Spencer's Autistic parent, Mama, responds to conflict in the Kimbell home. Sid was not punished for having a meltdown. Instead, they were heard and believed. Spencer disagreed with the suggestion she only use her mixer when Sid wasn't around. Mama valued Spencer's opinion and, ultimately, the family was able to come up with a better solution that everyone was happy with. With ear defenders and close adult supervision, both children were able to coexist with the mixer on.

I hope that caregivers, teachers and therapists of all neurotypes enjoy this story as much as their children do. I also hope you will join me and the other folks demanding better Autistic representation and more respectful strategies for working through conflict with neurodivergent children. Love, light and solidarity,

CPSIA information can be obtained
at www.ICGtesting.com
Printed in the USA
LVHW070742250322
714351LV00001B/4

9 798985 663105